DET ZACK

Mystery on the Midway

JERRY D. THOMAS

Pacific Press Publishing Association
Boise, Idaho
Oshawa, Ontario, Canada

Edited by Aileen Andres Sox
Designed by Dennis Ferree
Cover and inside art by Kim Justinen

ISBN 0-8163-1350-4

96 97 98 99 00 • 5 4 3 2 1

Dedication

To all the Zack friends I met this summer
at reading camp, at camp meetings,
at bookstores, and at book shows.
Thanks for helping me with ideas for this story
and for being patient until it was finished!

A special thanks to Jeremy
for reading the story first
and helping me tell it just right.

Other books by
Jerry D. Thomas

Detective Zack and the Secret in the Storm
Detective Zack Danger at Dinosaur Camp
Detective Zack and the Missing Manger Mystery
Detective Zack and the Mystery at Thunder Mountain
Detective Zack and the Red Hat Mystery
Detective Zack and the Secret in the Sand
Detective Zack and the Secret of Noah's Flood

Contents

CHAPTER ONE

Llama on the Loose

There are tooth marks all over my pencil. One corner of my notebook is nearly chewed off. And I'm surrounded by chickens.

This was supposed to be an easy job.

When Dusty and I offered to help Grandma show her prize chickens at the county fair, we thought it would just take a few minutes to carry the cage in. Then we'd be off to watch them set up the Ferris wheel and the carousel.

Boy, were we wrong. I've been pecked on, chewed on, stepped on, and drug through stuff I hope was mud. Now I'm sitting here in this big barn, surrounded by straw and wire cages. All around me are hundreds of chickens, ducks, geese, and turkeys—and none of them are being quiet!

It all started when Dusty and I walked into the poultry and small animal barn, carrying the cage with Grandma's two hens inside. This is kind of a small fair, so the chickens and other poultry were in the same barn with the rabbits, hamsters, and guinea pigs.

"Be careful," Grandma reminded us as we lifted the cage out of Grandpa's truck. "I don't have many chickens left, you know."

Boy, did I ever know! The hurricane that blew away her chickens almost blew me away too. And that was only a few weeks ago. My mom and dad came back to help fix some of the things the hurricane broke. There's so much to do, Grandma wasn't even going to show her prize chickens here at the county fair this year.

"We'll help," my sister Kayla and I told her.

"Me, too," our cousin Dusty chimed in. His family was back to help also.

Grandma smiled at us. "It's really not too difficult," she said. "Mostly, I'd need someone who would get Agatha and Esmeralda settled, then be around to give them food and water until the day they are judged."

"We can do that," I said with a smile. I could already see us dropping the two chickens off at their barn and spending the rest of the fair days hanging around the midway, playing games and riding rides.

So there I was, backing through the doorway into the small animal barn, carrying the front half of a cage with Agatha and Esmeralda cackling inside. My notebook was sitting on top of their cage—I knew there would be things to see as soon as we had them in place.

There was a lot going on in the doorway—two other kids were trying to lead a goose through with a leash and a collar, and the girl behind them had at least four rabbits in her arms. Maybe I was thinking too hard about what a Ferris wheel looks like while they put it up. Maybe I just wasn't listening. Anyway, the only warning I had was from Dusty. He didn't say anything, but his eyes got real big.

"What is it?" I asked. I had to stop backing up, because he stopped walking forward. Before he could answer, something hit me in the back. At the same time, a girl screamed, the goose started flapping and honking, and someone starting shouting.

Then I heard the loudest noise of all. It sounded like it was right by my ear.

Blaat!

I spun around and stared right into a big hairy face with long lips. I tried to step back, but the goose had wrapped its leash around my legs. I fell backwards and ended up flat on the floor with Agatha and Esmeralda right in my lap—still in their cage, luckily.

Before I could think, there was another loud noise in my ear. This time it was someone shouting. "Zack! Help!"

I twisted my neck to look. A girl in dirty clothes was laying on the floor beside me, hanging on to a rope. It was my sister, Kayla!

"Help!" she shouted, like I was deaf or something. "I can't make him stop!"

Then she started sliding out the door. Before I could move, a rabbit hopped right across my chest. I looked up and saw Dusty just standing there. His eyes were still big, but his mouth was even bigger. It was hanging open like a cave.

"Dusty, get these chickens off me!" I shouted. I had to shout because the goose was honking and hissing at me so loud. "Hey, I wasn't the one who tripped *you*," I said to the goose as his two owners tried to calm him down.

Finally, Dusty pulled and I pushed and we slid our cageful of squawking chickens onto the ground. The girl who used to have four rabbits now only had two, and she was crying her eyes out. Dusty took off after a pair of long ears showing behind the door and the girl followed.

I tried to calm the chickens. "Now, Esmeralda, you're not hurt. Settle down." She just stared at me with her beady eyes and clucked a few things I'm glad I couldn't understand. I jumped up and headed out the door. "Dusty, keep an eye on the chickens!" I shouted over my shoulder.

Outside, Kayla was sliding along in the dirt. But now I could see why—the other end of her rope was tied around the neck of a hairy-faced, long-lipped llama! I raced after them and caught up when the llama stopped to sniff a flower.

"Whoa," I said, grabbing the llama's rope about a foot from its head. "Hold on for a second. Kayla, what are you doing?"

Kayla stood up and tried to brush the dirt off her pants. She should have started with her face—it was just as dirty. "What am I doing!" she almost shouted. "I was just trying to help! I wish I knew what this maniac animal thinks it's doing. It drug me right out of the large animal barn and right through the small animal barn."

"But..." I tried to ask a question, but Kayla was just getting started.

"Look at my jeans! And my shirt! Do you have

any idea what I was drug through?"Based on the smell coming from her general direction, I could make a pretty good guess. I didn't have the heart to tell her what her face looked like. "Kayla, how did you get on the other end of this rope?"

When I raised the rope up, the llama decided it was time to move on. I planted my feet and pulled back. It was strong!

"Oh, no, you don't," Kayla said. She grabbed the end of the rope and pulled too. Together, we barely kept the llama from moving. "It belongs to . . . oh, here they are."

A man and a woman ran up to us, both talking at the same time—sometimes to us and sometimes to the llama. "Are you OK? Leonard, you bad llama! Where did you think you were going? Thank you for stopping him—he's such a stubborn thing. Just look at what he did to you!"

By now, the woman was brushing the dirt off Kayla's pants. "Let me help," she said. She reached into her pocket. "I think I have a handkerchief for your face."

"My face?" Kayla repeated. "What's wrong with my face?" She looked at me.

I shrugged. "It's not really that bad. Just a little dirt—and stuff." For some reason, she screamed and ran toward the restrooms.

The man grabbed onto Leonard's rope. I was happy to let go. "Thanks a lot," he said. "Come by the llama pens later. I want to give you two something for all your trouble."

"OK, sure," I answered as they led their llama away. *I might go*, I thought, *but Kayla will never want to see a llama again as long as she lives.*

When I got back inside the barn, Dusty had rounded up the two missing rabbits and calmed down the chickens. "What happened?" he asked. "What was that—a camel?"

I told him about Leonard. "He got away from some people over in the other barn. Kayla grabbed his rope, but she couldn't stop him." Before I could finish, someone ran between us and started talking. It was Sonia, Kayla's friend. She lives on the farm next to our grandparents. She's the one I rescued during the hurricane.

"Where's Kayla? Have you seen Zippy?"

I stepped back. "Kayla's in the restroom—Zippy who?"

Sonia grabbed both my arms. "We have to find Zippy! Help me!"

Before I could say a word, she saw Kayla coming through the door behind me. "Come on," she shouted past my head. "Zippy's gone. We have to find him!"

"Zippy who?" I repeated. But they both ignored me and raced toward the other end of the barn. Then Kayla turned and looked back.

"Come on, Zack," she called. "Help us find Zippy!"

I looked at Dusty. He just shrugged his shoulders and stared after them.

"Who's Zippy?" we both shouted.

CHAPTER TWO

The Search for Zippy

I still don't think it was my fault that Officer Chan got mad at us. When Sonia and Kayla dashed out the barn door, we ran after them. And I ran right into Officer Chan.

"Whoa," he said with a smile. "I came down to investigate a runaway llama and all I've found so far are runaway boys. What's the big rush?"

I pointed outside. "My sister's friend lost someone."

"You mean she lost her own parents?"

Dusty shook his head. "She lost someone she was watching—someone named Zippy."

He pushed the barn door open. "Show me where she is."

Dusty led the way out, then stopped. "I don't see Sonia or Kayla, Zack. Where did they lose him?"

"Around this side," I said, pointing to the left. "I heard Sonia say that he may have gone into the bushes." We found them right around the corner.

"Come on, Zack—help us," Kayla called. She had her head stuck in the leaves of a big green bush. "Come here, Zippy," she shouted into the bush. "Come back to us."

Officer Chan pushed forward. "How old is Zippy?" he asked, pulling a pen and notepad out of his pocket.

Sonia pulled her head out of another bush and answered. "He's almost two years old. He's so little—I know he must be scared to death!"

Officer Chan whipped out his radio. It crackled to life. "Headquarters, we have a situation here by the small animal barn."

A voice responded quickly. "Go ahead, Officer Chan."

He continued. "We have a missing two-year-old male. He has been missing for almost ten minutes. Send all available officers to assist."

The voice on the radio sounded very serious. "Understood, Officer Chan. All available officers, assist in the search for a missing child near the small animal barn."

Officer Chan clipped the radio back to his belt. "Where did you see him last?" he asked Sonia.

Sonia looked at Kayla. Kayla stared back. They both looked confused. Officer Chan tried another question. "Who is responsible for little Zippy?"

"I am," Sonia answered. "But . . ."

Officer Chan interrupted. "So, he's your little brother?"

Kayla laughed out loud. Sonia almost fell over. "No!" she shouted. "He's my hamster!"

Then Officer Chan turned to me. "You said they were looking for a kid."

I held up my hands. "That's what I thought! We asked them who Zippy was, didn't we, Dusty?"

Dusty nodded. "We both asked and all they said was, 'Help us find him.'"

Both Kayla and Sonia starting telling their story at once. Of course, Dusty and I had to explain our side. Before long, Officer Chan was waving his arms and shouting too.

His voice was loudest. "Just a moment! Let's be quiet for just a moment, please!" When we stopped, he pulled out his radio. "Headquarters, cancel the call for help on a missing child." Then he stared at us. "If you kids were playing a joke, it wasn't funny. A lost child is a very serious matter."

Sonia explained again. "When that llama ran

past me, Zippy slipped out of my hands. I know he was supposed to be in a cage, but he gets scared around lots of people. And now . . ." Sonia suddenly remembered that Zippy was still missing. "Now he must be scared to death! Please let us go find him."

The tears in Sonia's eyes seemed to melt the frown on Officer Chan's face. "OK. You keep looking. As soon as I make sure that llama is in its pen, I'll come and help."

Sonia turned and ran along the edge of the animal building. Kayla headed back into the bushes. "Thank you," Dusty called as Officer Chan hurried away. Then he turned to me. "So, what do we do now? Agatha and Esmeralda are still sitting on the floor back there."

"We'd better take care of them," I agreed. "Kayla, we'll be right back," I shouted. She shouted something to us, but we didn't wait to find out what.

As quickly as we could, we got the chickens settled in their spot and promised to be back with their food and water soon. Esmeralda just gave me that beady-eyed stare, like she didn't believe a word I said.

Just as we caught up with the girls, I heard a scream. Down by the row of booths and tents, a woman was standing on a table. "That was the biggest rat I've ever seen!" she complained loudly. "Someone call security and tell them to get that thing out of here!"

"Sounds like a lot of animals are running loose today," Dusty said. He turned to look behind some trash cans, but I grabbed his arm.

"Dusty, do you think that woman could have seen something that looked like a big rat, but wasn't really a rat at all?"

"Huh?" Dusty didn't get it.

I put my hands up to mouth and shouted past his head. "Sonia, come quick!"

Sonia popped up from behind a trailer. "Did you find Zippy?"

"Maybe," I said. "Come on." While the four of us ran, I explained. "What if she saw Zippy and thought he was a big rat?"

It wasn't hard to find the woman who had screamed. She was still on the table. "Excuse me," I said. "What did the rat look like?"

She shivered. "It was big and ugly."

Sonia held her hands out. "Was it about this big? With lots of fuzzy brown hair?"

The woman thought, then nodded. "You know, it was the fuzziest rat I've ever seen."

"It was Zippy!" Sonia cried. "It was my hamster!"

"A hamster?" The woman put her hands on her hips. "Well, that's different." She climbed back down to the ground. "I think he was going that way." She pointed off to the right, farther down the row of tents and booths.

Sonia walked along behind the little buildings, calling Zippy quietly. We walked along the road in front. Or at least, we tried to. People were moving things into each booth—all kinds of things. We stepped carefully around a display of wind chimes, each one pinging a different tune in the breeze.

"Hi, kids," a man called from behind a counter in his big, open-sided building. "Don't forget to stop by after we're open. You'll love this corn-on-the-cob."

We just smiled and kept going. As we walked past a tent selling belt buckles and baseball cards, an ice cream shop in a trailer, and a radio station inside a little wooden booth, Kayla shook her head. "This place is going to be like a little mall—except everything is outside."

"We're never going to find him," Sonia moaned from behind a yellow-striped tent. Since no one was in the tent, we stopped and looked around the stacks of boxes and tables. No Zippy.

"Come on," Kayla said, pulling Sonia toward the door. "Let's keep going."

Dusty walked out backward so he could talk to Sonia. "You think Zippy might go down there where the rides are?" he asked in kind of a hopeful way. "There is a lot of grass under that spot where they're putting up—Ooof!"

Before any of us could say a word, Dusty backed right into a boy about our age who was rushing by. They both stumbled and fell.

"Yikes!" Dusty exclaimed as he hit the dirt. He turned and looked for what he had run into. "Are you OK?" he asked when he saw the other kid on the ground too.

The kid seemed fine once he got his black baseball cap back on. He stood up and brushed off his pants without ever letting go of the dirty yellow-and-white-striped bag he was holding tightly. "Sorry," he mumbled as he turned and almost ran toward the rides.

"Hey, it was my fault," Dusty called after him.

"He didn't seem very friendly," Kayla said. "I wonder what he's in a hurry about."

Sonia didn't care. "I know *we* should be in a hurry—to find Zippy. Come on!"

We all followed her, but I kept watching the boy in the black cap. He turned and looked back at us three times. *Why is he so interested in us*, I wondered. *And what does he have in that bag?*

DETECTIVE ZACK

Maybe something we're looking for?

Finally, Sonia collapsed against the wall of the last booth in the row. "We're never going to find Zippy," she moaned. "I just know it."

Before any of us could say anything, another voice spoke. "I see you have lost something— something very important to you. I can help you find it."

The voice came from above us. And just over Sonia's head was a window. A blue glass statue of an angel stood just inside. And right behind the angel was a woman—wearing a scarf on her head, gold earrings as big as bracelets in her ears, and a smile.

CHAPTER THREE

Madame LaTonn

We all stood up and stared for a minute. Dusty read the sign on the front of the booth. "Blue Angel Answers," he read. "Need advice? Help? Hints about your future? Or about your love life? Let the power of angels work for you."

And right below that was a smaller sign that told us who had spoken. It said, "Madame LaTonn—Answers, Three Dollars."

Kayla was reading too. "The power of angels?" she whispered to me. "I didn't know angels did things like that for people."

Sonia wasn't worried about that. "Are you Madame LaTonn?" The woman nodded. "Did you say you could find Zippy?" Sonia asked.

Madame LaTonn laughed softly. "No, child. I cannot. But an angel can." She reached her hands out to the statue of the blue angel and touched it lightly. "Angels have the power to do many things."

That made my eyebrows go up. I wasn't sure I understood exactly what I was hearing. "Do you mean that angels know Zippy ran away and got lost and that they know where he is right now?" I asked.

Madame LaTonn turned and stared right at me. "Don't you know that angels are all around us? They are here to protect us, to help us, and to teach us. Haven't you learned about angels in church?"

"Well, yes," I said.

"And if the angels have been around you children all day, then they know what has happened. And how to find what you have lost." Her smile made it seem like a simple thing everyone should know.

Sonia reached into her pocket. "Here's my three dollars, Madame LaTonn. Please ask the angels where Zippy is."

Madame LaTonn waved her hand. "I will not take your money, my dear. But I will ask for you."

Dusty was still confused. "Who are you going to ask? That blue angel?"

"Shhh. Quiet, please," Madame LaTonn said as she closed her eyes and wrapped her hands around the angel.

As she stood without moving, I looked around the inside of her booth. On each wall, a whole shelf was lined with tiny blue glass angels—all for sale. Just behind where Madame LaTonn stood a blue curtain was drawn across the little booth. I knew there was a door in the back, because it opened and sunlight streamed in behind the curtain. Then it closed quickly and the room was dark again. But only for a few seconds—then something strange started to happen.

"Oh!" Sonia exclaimed. Then she slapped one hand over her mouth and used the other to point at the blue angel.

The angel was glowing! I could just barely tell at first, but the glow got brighter and brighter.

"Zack, do you see that?" Kayla whispered.

"Shhh!" Sonia hissed.

Suddenly, the glow disappeared. Madame LaTonn opened her eyes and looked at Sonia. "The angel says, 'What you are looking for is in a small dark place, in a large bright place striped in yellow.'"

Sonia stared at her. "What? What does that mean? Is that all?"

Madame LaTonn held out her hands. "That is all the angel told me. I cannot explain. I hope you find what you are looking for." With that, she pulled the window closed and disappeared behind the curtain.

Sonia slumped to the ground again. "We'll never find Zippy now. What was that supposed to mean—a dark place, a light place, a yellow place? What kind of angel would tell you a weird thing like that?"

The whole angel thing seemed weird to me, but it still made me think of something. "Wait a minute," I said. "She didn't say a yellow place. She said a bright place striped with yellow."

Kayla was getting it too. "Like that one tent we went in—it was white with yellow stripes, right?"

Sonia was on her feet. "The tent! Let's go!"

"Wait," I said. "It might be a different tent. Or something else that's got yellow stripes." But Sonia was already running and dragging Kayla along with her. "Come on," I said to Dusty. "Let's go."

The tent was a good place to look. But I was thinking about a yellow-striped bag and a boy wearing a black baseball cap.

Guess who met us right in front of the yellow tent? Officer Chan. "Any luck finding your—Hold on!" He held out his hand as Sonia tried to rush past him into the tent. "I'm sure the owners of that stuff don't want any kids messing around with it."

Sonia was nearly in tears again. "But we have to look in there. That's where the angel said we would find Zippy!"

"Wait a minute." Now Officer Chan was confused. "An angel told you where to find your missing hamster?"

Dusty pointed back the way we had come. "The blue angel—and the strange woman. What was her name—Mrs. LaTongue?"

Officer Chan nodded. "Madame LaTonn. I've met her." He looked around at us. "And you believe she knows where your hamster is hiding?"

"Yes, yes!" Sonia said.

I shrugged.

"We don't know where else to look," Kayla added.

After a second or two, Office Chan sighed and shook his head. "OK. But I'll be going with you. I don't want any more booth operators thinking some kids are trying to steal their things."

Inside the tent looked the same as before. The stacks of boxes and tables were still there. "What else did the angel say?" Sonia asked.

I thought for a second. "'A small dark place

inside a big, light place.' If this is the bright place, where is the small dark one?"

One look around told me that there was only one answer. Kayla said it first. "Under a box!"

"Ugh," Dusty grunted. "Not a heavy one, I hope."

Sonia ignored him and reached for the nearest box. "Wait a minute," Office Chan said. "If boxes need to be touched or moved, I'll do the touching or moving. And we will not be opening any boxes to look inside."

He reached for the nearest stack of boxes. This time, I stopped him. "No," I said suddenly. "Pick up that one." I pointed to a box sitting alone on the grass. Looking at the letters on its side, I could tell the box was upside down.

Officer Chan nodded, then stepped over and grabbed it. When he picked it up, it was so light, I knew it was empty.

Empty except for one thing. One fuzzy brown thing about as big as a big rat.

CHAPTER FOUR

Corn-on-the-Cob and Questions

The fuzzy pile of brown fur was our missing hamster.

"Zippy!" Sonia cried. She had her hands around him before anyone else could blink. "Oh, Zippy, I was so scared for you. Are you OK?"

Officer Chan smiled. "It looks like Madame LaTonn knew right where it was."

"No," Sonia insisted. "An angel did."

Even now, sitting here by Grandma's chickens with my notebook, I can't say that Sonia was wrong. I'm not sure she was right either, but maybe there are things about angels that I don't know. So now you know why I'm writing in my notebook this time. I have questions that need answers. What do angels do for people? What does the Bible say about angels?

I wasn't the only one with a brain full of questions. Kayla helped us get food and water for the chickens when we got back to the barn. And by the look on her face, she felt just as confused as I did.

"Zack," she asked, "do you think Madame LaTonn really asked an angel where to find Zippy?"

Dusty had been thinking too. "What about that blue angel statue? What was that glowing about? Do you think that's when the angel was talking to her?"

Before I could add any of my questions, Grandma and Mom arrived. "Well, it looks like you have these chickens all settled," Grandma said. She moved over close to the cage and bent down to speak. "How are you feeling, Agatha? And you, Esmeralda? Let's not get nervous and start losing feathers, girls."

Esmeralda stepped over close to Grandma. *Baaaawk—bock—bock*, she squawked, turning her head back and forth.

I just knew she was trying to tell Grandma all about the day—getting dropped to the ground and left there, going without food and water for more than a few minutes. And I just knew she was blaming it all on me!

32

Mom was watching too. "Look at that," she said to Kayla. "Sometimes I think your grandmother can actually understand those chickens."

"Not this time, I hope," I mumbled.

Grandma stood up—and smiled at me. "You boys did a good job." She held out some money. "Why don't you go get something to eat while I find out when they'll be judging the chickens."

"Thanks, Grandma," Dusty said. "Come on, Zack. Let's go find some french fries."

I grabbed his arm. "Wait a minute, Dusty. I think I want corn-on-the-cob. Kayla, are you coming with us?"

Mom liked that idea. "Corn sounds like a good healthy snack. Kayla, go with them if you'd like. I want to tag along with Grandma."

Just by the sounds, I could tell that the fair was open. Instead of trucks and forklifts and hammers, it sounded like people. People were screaming as they whirled around on the Tilt-O-Whirl on the midway. The little roller coaster was *clack-clack-clacking* around its track. And from all over came the sounds of voices—laughing, shouting, talking, or singing.

As we walked along the roadway, there were people already shopping at the booths on both sides. "Hey, why did you suddenly want corn?"

Dusty asked. "I still want french fries."

"Because the corn-on-the-cob place is close to Madame LaTonn," I reminded them. "And I still have a lot of questions about her and her angels."

Kayla snapped her fingers. "Good idea! Maybe we can get close enough to hear what she says to someone else."

By the time we got our food and sat down at the table nearest Madame LaTonn's booth, three people were waiting to ask her a question. "We're not close enough to hear anything," Kayla grumbled.

Suddenly Dusty pointed. "Look! The blue light!" He tried to whisper, but ended up spraying corn bits all over the table. "Sorry," he added.

We watched until the woman who had been talking to Madame LaTonn walked away. She looked confused, but she was smiling. Next, a man and a woman stepped up. After the blue light and a few words from Madame LaTonn, they walked toward us, laughing.

"What was that supposed to mean?" the man asked as they waited in line for corn. He tried to make his voice sound like Madame LaTonn's. "'Your future has black and white and music. And many four-footed creatures.'"

"Hey, maybe the angel was talking about our

wedding," the woman answered. "You know—
black tuxedos, white dress, the wedding music.
We are still getting married, right?"

"Of course," he said. "But what about the creatures? Are you planning to have dogs in the
wedding?"

She laughed. "No. Maybe it means we'll have a
horse farm someday."

The man rolled his eyes. "Maybe it means our
house will be full of mice! These fortune-tellers
are all alike."

Before we could hear anything else, someone
behind us started shouting. "Hey, someone stole
my camera!"

I turned to see a large man waving his arms and
shouting at the man behind the counter in the
corn-on-the-cob booth. "I set it down right there
on that table while I was ordering. And now it's
gone!"

By now, everyone was staring. The corn man
leaned out past the corner and talked more quietly. "I'll call security. You just wait there to tell
them what happened. Here, have another piece of
corn." As he picked up a walkie-talkie, he kept
talking to himself. "I was afraid this would keep
happening," he said.

Because I was watching the corn man, I saw

someone on the other side of the booth duck down and walk away quickly. I barely had time to see who it was.

"Come on," I as I stood up and dropped my cob in the big trash can. "Let's go. We've got someone to follow."

Kayla dropped hers in the trash, too, but Dusty was still chewing on his ear of corn. "I'm not done yet," he said.

"Bring it with you," I called over my shoulder. I didn't want to get too far behind.

"Who are we following?" Kayla asked.

I pointed ahead. "The kid with the black baseball cap. He ducked away from there as soon as the corn man started calling security."

"Is that the same kid I ran into?" Dusty asked between bites. I nodded and led the way around a booth full of little kids getting cat whiskers and stuff painted on their faces. The baseball cap kid was a long way ahead of us and heading straight toward the games and rides on the midway.

"Do you think he stole the camera?" Kayla hissed in my ear.

I kept my eyes on him. "Maybe. I think he's carrying that bag again—the same yellow striped one he had earlier. He could be hiding something inside."

He slowed down near the Ferris wheel and we caught up. Then he ducked behind the row of game booths. I waved for the others to follow and ran far enough to stick my head around the back corner where he had gone.

Kayla's head bumped mine as she tried to see too. "Where is he?" she whispered. Then we both saw him. As we watched, he stopped by the door to the back of the basketball hoop game booth. Then he stood still for a few seconds, like he was listening or looking for something.

"What is he doing?" Dusty asked.

"I don't know," I whispered. I couldn't hear anything but those basketballs smacking against the backboard of the game. Finally, he looked both ways, then slid the door open and stepped inside.

"So he is the thief," I said. "Come on." I didn't wait to look or listen before I yanked the door open. Maybe I should have.

Angel Clues

Do angels really answer questions for people? And help us find things we lost if we ask them to?

Where did that blue light that made the angel glow come from?

How else could Madame LaTonn know where Zippy was? Maybe it really was an angel.

Words to remember

Midway: The main road at a carnival or fair, where the games and rides are.

Midway Mystery

Who stole the camera? Why did the corn man say it was happening again?

The kid in the black cap left as soon as it happened. Maybe he's the thief.

CHAPTER FIVE

A Carny Kid

Now that I'm sitting here watching the chickens again, I'm sure we should have looked around and waited a few seconds yesterday before we went in the back door of that basketball hoop game. It's always easier to know what you should have done after you already did something else.

Anyway, this is turning into a bigger mystery than I thought.

When I stepped through that door, the kid in the black cap did exactly what a guilty person would do. He whirled around and when he saw us, he started backing toward the curtain that led to the game. "Hey, what are you guys doing here?"

"We were going to ask you the same question,"

I answered. But before I could say anything else, a tall woman wearing a basketball warm-up suit stepped through the curtain and bumped into the kid. He almost jumped out of his skin.

"Hold on, there," the woman said as she grabbed him by one arm. Then she looked at us. "Who are you?"

Before I could answer, someone knocked on the door once, then yanked it open. It was Officer Chan! For a second, I was happy. *Now we can just tell him about the kid sneaking in here.* Then I realized something else. *We snuck in here just like he did. He might accuse us of trying to steal from the basketball game lady.*

"Pardon me, Mrs. Davis," he said to the woman. "Is everything OK this evening?"

She kind of glared at him. "Officer, you weren't following my son and his friends, were you?"

Kayla turned at stared at me. She must have been thinking what I was thinking. *The kid with the black cap is her son? Now we are in trouble for sure. He'll tell them we aren't his friends, that we snuck in after him.*

Officer Chan smiled. "Just trying to make sure there are no problems. That's my job, after all."

Mrs. Davis looked at her son. "Well, Donovan, are there any problems?"

I held my breath. Donovan looked at us again, then shook his head. Mrs. Davis turned back to Officer Chan. "No problems, officer. Thanks for stopping by."

As Officer Chan left, Mrs. Davis headed back through the curtain. "I'd love to stay and chat, kids, but I've got customers who want to spend money."

Then we were alone with the kid we had followed, the kid we thought was the thief. "Hi, Donovan," I said. "I'm Zack. This is my cousin, Dusty, and my sister, Kayla. Why didn't you tell your mom that you don't even know us?"

Donovan kind of grinned and shrugged. "I guess I was hoping that we would be friends. I saw you guys around today and you were always doing something. I don't have many friends since we move so much, and since none of the other carnies have kids my age."

"None of the other *whos*?" Kayla asked.

"None of the other carnies," Donovan repeated. "A carny is a person who works in a carnival or fair like this one. They travel with the fair from one town to the next, setting up the rides and the game booths."

I nodded. "So your mom's a carny."

"So's my dad," he added. "He's in charge of

setting up and taking down everything. And he runs the Ferris wheel."

"Wow!" Dusty was impressed. "You must be able to ride it every night."

"I guess I could," Donovan agreed. "But it's kind of boring to ride alone. You guys want to ride it now?"

Dusty jumped up. "Let's go!"

As we walked along the midway, Donovan waved to the people behind the counters of each game. "Hey, Donovan," one man called, "bring your friends over for a try at Ring-Toss. Everyone's a winner!"

Kayla stopped. "That could be fun."

Donovan shook his head as he waved at the man. "Don't go there. Mr. Connelly will find a way to make you lose your money."

Kayla wasn't convinced. "But he said 'everyone's is winner'."

Donovan nodded. "Everyone does win—a prize that's worth about ten cents. Of course, you have to pay fifty cents to play. And he'll talk you into trying a shot at tossing the ring farther away. Hardly anyone ever wins his real prizes." He lowered his voice to whisper. "We think he cheats."

"Someone told me that all these games cheat you," Dusty said as we kept walking toward the Ferris wheel.

"Hey," Donovan said. "My mom doesn't cheat people. The basketball hoops are smaller than usual and everything, but you can see that before you play. It has to be hard to win, or the games would go out of business paying for all the prizes."

"You're right," Dusty said. "Besides, I'm saving all my money for the rides." He led the way to the gate in front of the spinning Ferris wheel. Donovan stepped around him.

"Hey, Dad!" he called over the noise of the carousel next door. "Can my friends and I have a ride?"

The man who answered looked big and strong enough to be spinning the Ferris wheel with one hand. "Sure, Donovan. We're not busy yet and this ride's nearly over. I'll get you on in just a minute."

"Wow," I said to Donovan, "your dad looks really strong!"

Donovan smiled proudly. "He is. You should see him when it's time to take down the rides. Mom says he can do more work than any other two men."

"OK," Donovan's dad called when the Ferris wheel was finally stopped. "Here you go. Only two in each chair. No funny business—no standing up or throwing things."

Donovan and I took the first chair and rose slowly as people got on and off. He pointed out the barns and I told him about the chickens. "I saw you in the small animal barn," Donovan replied. "I wondered which animal you were there with."

Before I could say anything else, Donovan took a deep breath and asked, "Why were you guys following me? What were you going to say before my mom showed up?"

I laughed. "Well, we didn't know that it was your mother's game booth. I thought you were sneaking in to take something. We were going to stop you and tell the person in charge of the game booth."

Donovan had to smile about that. "I could just see the look on Mom's face if you told her that someone was stealing from the booth, and then pointed to me. She'd have a fit!"

I decided to tell him more. "Did you hear that guy at the corn booth shouting about his stolen camera?"

"I sure did," Donovan said. "That's why I left so fast. I didn't want anyone to think I stole it."

"That's why I thought maybe you did it," I explained. "Because you left so fast. Then when you snuck in behind a game booth, I was almost sure. Now, I'm sure I was wrong."

We went up a little higher. Donovan kicked his feet until his shoe nearly fell off. "I thought that maybe you three had stolen that camera. That's why I was so shocked when you burst into the game booth room. I thought maybe you had come to steal our stuff too. "

"Thanks again for claiming us as your friends," I said. "It really would have been hard to explain what we thought to your mom and to Officer Chan."

Donovan turned and stared off into the distance. "Not as hard as you think," he mumbled.

Words to Remember

Carny: A person who travels with a carnival or fair, setting up and running the rides and the game booths.

Midway Mystery

Donovan says he's not the thief. I believe him. But who is?

_____
_____
_____
_____
_____
_____
_____
_____
_____
_____
_____
_____
_____
_____
_____
_____
_____
_____

CHAPTER SIX

Chickens and Angels

Esmeralda is giving me that look again. Like it's my fault she's not back in the barnyard scratching up bugs. I've been trying to tell her to blame Grandma. "She's the one who wants you to win a blue ribbon."

Baaawk-bock-bock.

"Hey," I said, "Dusty's coming with some new food. It's not my fault you tipped your dish over while I was cleaning your cage."

Baaawk. Esmeralda was sure it was my fault.

"Why can't you just lay down and sleep like Agatha there?" Agatha opened one eye just long enough to glare at me.

Personally, I think they're both spoiled.

DETECTIVE ZACK

Last night was really fun. Donovan knows everyone who works at the fair. I'm glad he wants to be friends. We got to ride the Ferris wheel three times in a row! It's a great place to spy from.

The sun was almost down when we got on, but in the fading light, I could see all over the fairgrounds. The lights were coming on and the midway was shining brighter than a Christmas tree. When we got to the top, Donovan pointed toward the back of the fairgrounds. "That's where we live," he said as a large group of small travel trailer houses came into view. "All the carnies live out in that field. That big green trailer is ours."

"Hey, look," Dusty called from the next chair. "Is that blue light Madame LaTonn's angel?"

"No, silly," Kayla said, elbowing him a little. "That's a street light."

That made me think of something I wanted to ask Donovan. "Do you know Madame LaTonn? The woman with the blue angel?"

"Sure. Everyone knows her. She's at most of the same fairs we are."

That surprised me. "Is she a carny too?" I asked.

Donovan snorted. "No way. Carnies do all the work. She just rents a booth space. Someone else must set it up for her."

"Donovan, do you believe in Madame LaTonn's angels?"

The smile on his face told me the answer before he said a word. "Oh, yes. I believe they are real. She does wonderful things for people because of the angels." He looked at me kind of strangely. "I heard that she helped you today. Don't you believe in her angels?"

"Yeess," I answered slowly. "The whole thing just seems a little strange. Do a lot of people ask her for answers?"

"Her Blue Angel booth almost always has a line of people. Lots of carnies ask her questions—I've even seen Mr.Connelly there."

That kind of surprised me. "Do people always find what they're looking for, or get the answer they need?"

This time, Donovan answered slowly. "Well, not always. The messages she gives are not always easy to understand. I'm not sure everyone is happy with her answers. But some are."

I swatted at a June bug that was buzzing by. "Why are her answers so strange? It seems like if you wanted to help someone, you'd give a plain answer."

Donovan defended her. "Hey, she can only tell us what the angel tells her. That's all she ever says—she never tries to explain it."

I remembered that. "So why do the angels answer with riddles we have to figure out? Is that some kind of test to see if we deserve help?"

Donovan waved the question away. "Maybe that's just the way angels are. I believe that angels are around us all the time. It just takes someone special like Madame LaTonn to talk to them and listen to them."

With all these questions about angels whirling around in my head, I decided to talk to Mom last night. She was sitting out on the porch swing, listening to the bug-zapper french fry some mosquitos. "Mom?" I asked, "can I ask you something?"

"Sure, Zack." She patted the seat beside her. "Come sit beside me and ask away."

I didn't waste any time. "Mom, do you believe in angels?"

She stared and blinked like Esmeralda for a second. "Of course, Zack. You know I do. Where does this question come from?"

I didn't want to tell her about Madame LaTonn yet. "My friend Donovan believes that angels are around us all the time."

Mom nodded. "Donovan is your friend from the fair, right?"

"Right. He says angels are always there to help us, but only a few special people actually know how to talk to them and listen to them. Those people can get help finding things or answering questions straight from an angel."

"What do you think?" she asked.

"I'm not sure," I answered. "Angels helped people in the Bible, didn't they? And they did talk to people—at least they did in Bethlehem when Jesus was born."

"Zack, your questions don't have simple answers. We don't know much about angels. The Bible doesn't say a lot about them. But I think you need to find out what it does say. And I know just the tool for a detective with questions like yours. Wait here."

She went inside the house and came back with a book bigger than my Bible. "This is a concordance (con-core-dents)."

"A concordance?" I had to use both hands to take it from her. "Mom, my Bible's not even this big. Wouldn't it be faster just to read it?"

"A concordance is not a big book to read. It's a very useful tool." She opened it to the first page. "Look, it works like a dictionary. All the important words in the Bible are listed in alphabetical order."

DETECTIVE ZACK

I looked at the long list of words and names starting with "a." "Here's Abraham," I said pointing to the page. "Wow! I never knew his name showed up that many times."

She pointed to the end of a line. "Instead of telling you what each word means, a concordance tells you where that word is found in the Bible— all the places where it is used."

"I get it. At the end of each line is the verse where that word is used." I looked closely at Abraham again. "Most of the verses that use the word 'Abraham' are in Genesis. That makes sense—that's where his story is."

Mom smiled. "You can use the concordance to find any word in the Bible."

My head snapped up. "Angels!" Quickly, I turned the pages until I found the word. "Here's the list. Now all I have to do is look up each verse."

"No problem for a detective," Mom agreed. "Every one of those clues will tell you more about angels—and hopefully answer your questions."

So this morning, I have my notebook, my chewed-on pencil, a concordance, and two Bibles. After we get these chickens taken care of, Dusty and I are planning to get a giant dill pickle, find a table to sit at, and look up those angel verses.

At least that's what we were planning. Before

Kayla came crashing into the barn, shouting for me. "Zack, come on! That man whose camera was stolen is talking to Officer Chan. He's trying to blame some kids for stealing it. I think he might mean us!"

I took one step toward her, then stopped. "Sorry, girls," I said to the chickens. "I promise Dusty will be here soon with some food."

I know Esmeralda didn't believe a word I said.

Angel Clues

Why are Madame LaTonn's angel answers riddles? It could be some kind of test to see if the person is good enough to smart enough to be helped.

Do angels only talk to special people, like Madame LaTonn? It seems like they should talk to regular people, like they did in the Bible stories.

Words to Remember

Concordance: A big book that lists all the important words in the Bible. It tells which book and chapter and verse the word shows up in each time it does.

CHAPTER SEVEN

Number-One Suspect

"That was a good camera, and I hate to lose it."

"We're doing everything we can to find it."

Officer Chan and the man whose camera was stolen were standing right outside the barn door next to the hamsters and rabbits. Sonia was standing in the doorway listening. We slipped up next to her.

"Look, Officer, I can replace the camera. But I can't replace the pictures inside. There was only one shot left on the roll of film. We used most of it taking pictures at our family reunion last week. Some of those pictures are of family I hadn't seen for twenty years."

Officer Chan made a note on his pad. The man

kept talking. "I still think some kids took off with it. I mean, it wasn't an expensive camera. It wasn't even in a case. Probably they were just messing around, pressing the flash button about a hundred times. Then when the battery was dead, they dumped it in a trash can or behind some booth."

"We'll keep looking, Mr. Tedrow," Officer Chan said. "Maybe it will still turn up."

Suddenly, Sonia spoke up. "Why don't you ask Madame LaTonn where it is?"

"Who's she?" Mr. Tedrow asked Sonia.

"She has the Blue Angel booth by the midway. She told us exactly where to find my hamster when it was lost."

Mr. Tedrow looked at Officer Chan. "Blue Angel?"

Officer Chan shrugged. "For three dollars, she will ask an angel for the answer to whatever question you have. She claims that angels give her the answers."

"Is she ever right?"

"Sometimes," Officer Chan admitted. "But her answers are not very clear. Often, they could mean a hundred different things."

Mr. Tedrow looked back at Sonia, then made up his mind. "It's worth three dollars to try. Come on, young lady. Show me where this Blue Angel booth is."

Kayla and I and Officer Chan tagged along behind as Sonia led the way to Madame LaTonn's. The blue light snapped off just as we got there.

Madame LaTonn spoke to young woman who was waiting. "There is a church filled with flowers and music in your future."

"A wedding," the woman almost whispered. "I'm going to get married! I've got to tell Paul!"

Kayla smiled. "It sure sounded like a wedding to me."

"Or a funeral," Officer Chan pointed out. "Church, flowers, music?"

Kayla's smile disappeared.

Mr. Tedrow already had his money on the counter. "My camera was stolen right over there," he said to Madame LaTonn. "I need to find it. Can you tell me where it is?"

Madame LaTonn closed her eyes and wrapped her hands around the blue angel statue again. "Watch this," Sonia whispered to Mr. Tedrow. Slowly, light began to fill the blue angel until it was glowing like a lamp.

When the glow stopped, Madame LaTonn opened her eyes and stared at Mr. Tedrow. "What you have lost is in a field of big boxes, under the green."

Mr. Tedrow stared back. "What does that mean?"

Madame LaTonn stared even harder and answered. "You will find it under the big green box."

Mr. Tedrow nodded his head slowly. "OK. Thank you." Then he walked away. "You were right," he said to Officer Chan. "That wasn't much help. Anyway, thanks for what you are doing. You have my phone number." He started to leave, then stopped and turned to Kayla and me. "If you kids hear anything about the camera—or know anyone who does—tell them this: You can keep the camera. All I want back is the roll of film inside."

He left and I walked over to sit at one of the corn-on-the-cob tables. Sonia was the only one smiling as they followed me. "I'm sure we can figure it out if we try," she said. "Where's a field of boxes?"

I looked around. "I guess if you call the booths boxes, this whole place is filled with them. Are there any green booths?"

Officer Chan shook his head. "I believe that all the booths are painted white."

Sonia put her hands on her hips. "Well, I'm not giving up. I'm going to look for a green booth. Kayla, are you coming with me?"

Kayla sat down instead. "I'd better not. I told Mom I'd meet her at the barn in a few minutes."

Sonia waved and left.

Officer Chan slid into the seat across from us. "There's something I've been meaning to ask you two. What was going on the other night at the basketball booth?"

I looked at Kayla. She looked at me.

Officer Chan waved his hand. "I know you're friends with Donovan now. But you weren't then. Why did you barge into his mother's booth?"

I took a deep breath. "We had seen Donovan around two or three times that day. And he always acted strange—you know, sneaking by or running away. Like he was afraid he'd get caught or something."

"He acted like he was guilty of doing something wrong," Officer Chan stated.

"Right," I agreed. "Then, we were sitting here eating corn when Mr. Tedrow started shouting about his camera being stolen. At the same time, I saw Donovan on the other side of the corn booth. When he heard the shouting, he turned and walked away fast. And he was carrying a bag with something in it."

Officer Chan folded his hands. "So you think Donovan stole the camera."

"Well, I thought so. So we followed him all the way back to the basketball booth. When he snuck in the door, we were sure he'd gone in there to steal also. So we went in after him, hoping he would drop everything or make so much noise that the booth operator would come back there."

"Then you would tell the operator that he was stealing and they would hold him there until security came," Officer Chan finished. "So you didn't know that the operator was his mother."

"That was a big surprise," I said. "I was sure that Donovan would tell her and then you that we had broken in to steal things. But he said we were his friends. And before long, we were."

Officer Chan thought for a minute. "So you never saw what was in his bag?"

I shook my head. "No. He must have left it there in the booth."

Kayla jumped in. "We don't think he's the thief now. He seems too nice to do something like that."

Officer Chan looked at both of us. "This stolen camera is not the first thing missing. The man in charge of security at the last town told me that a number of items were stolen while the fair was there. And he informed me that security in the town before his told him the same thing."

I nodded. "So that means someone who travels with the fair is the thief. If it was a visitor to the fair, it wouldn't keep happening at every town. It has to be one of the carnies."

"Very good, Zack. There's a reason why I showed up at the basketball booth at the same time you guys did that night. I was following Donovan too. He's our number-one suspect."

CHAPTER EIGHT

Clues About Angels

"Do you really think Donovan is the thief?" Kayla asked as we walked back to the barn. "He seems like a normal person—like you and me."

I shook my head. "I don't know what to believe. I like Donovan too. But we really don't know him very well. He might steal things just for some excitement if he's the only kid around.

She nodded. "Even a fair wouldn't be much fun all by yourself. He's got to be really lonely and bored sometimes. If he's been around most of the time when something is stolen—like Officer Chan says— then maybe he is doing it. But if he is, then where are the stolen things going? If he took that camera home, his mother would know it wasn't his."

"Maybe she's in on it too," I guessed. "And his dad. Maybe they send him out to steal things and sell them for money." But I really couldn't believe that. "His dad is in charge of most of the carnies. Why would he do something that dumb and lose his job?"

Kayla stuck her nose up in the air. "Well, I've decided he didn't do it. There has to be some other explanation."

I wanted to say the same thing.

When we got to the chickens, Dusty had already taken care of the food and water. "Hey, where have you guys been?"

Kayla explained and told him what Madame LaTonn said.

"A field with big boxes," Dusty repeated. "'Under the green box.' It doesn't make any sense to me."

Before she could tell him anything else, Grandma and Mom arrived. "Hi, kids," Mom said. "Are you about ready to get out of here and go do something?"

I was ready to leave quickly—before Esmeralda squawked to Grandma and got me in trouble. "Let's go," I said, picking up my heavy backpack. "We have some clues to follow up on."

"What clues?" Dusty asked as we headed out.

"Clues about angels," I answered. "I'm still confused about Madame LaTonn and her angels. I want to know what angels really do for people. And there's only one place to look." I set my backpack down on the nearest picnic table, unzipped it, and pulled out a Bible. Kayla opened it and started reading.

"I'll go get the pickles," Dusty offered. "Kayla, do you want one?"

"Huh? Oh, sure," she answered. By the time he got back, Kayla had already found the angels in the Christmas story. "See, the angels talked to people then—they talked to the shepherds."

I wrote that down in my notebook, then grabbed my pickle.

"So, how are we going to find all the verses about angels," Dusty asked after a loud crunch. "We can't read the whole Bible this morning."

"We don't have to," I answered. Then I pulled the concordance out of my bag. "This is our secret weapon. It will tell us exactly where to find the clues we're looking for."

I explained how the concordance worked and we each picked a text to look up. I was looking for Psalm 91:11 when a voice interrupted.

"Hi, guys! What are you doing?" It was Donovan. Kayla looked at me. I smiled at Donovan. "We're looking for clues," I said. "We're trying to solve a mystery."

He came and sat down beside me. "You're trying to solve a mystery by looking in books? What kind of mystery is it?"

"It's sort of about Madame LaTonn," Dusty answered. "But mostly about angels. We're trying to find out if angels really do things like she says they do. Like answer questions and help people and stuff like that."

Donovan picked up my Bible. "We used to have one of these. It had pictures of Jesus with little kids. I really liked that Bible."

"Then help us," I said. "Look up Psalm 91:11."

He looked closely at the page it was open to. "How do I find that?"

I showed him the table of contents in the front. "This is what I always use when I can't find the book I'm looking for. See, it tells you the page number that Psalms starts on. When you get to that page, then you're at chapter one. You just keep turning pages until you find chapter 91."

Kayla was already at Psalm 148. "It's a long list of everything that God created. And it includes angels."

"OK," I said as I wrote, "God created the angels."

Dusty found Hebrews 1. "Hum. It says that angels are spirits who serve God. And that God sends them to help those who are following Him."

I wrote, "Angels serve God and God sends them to help us."

"I found Psalms!" Donovan said excitedly. Then he frowned. "Look how long it is. All the way to chapter 91, right?"

"Right," I answered.

Kayla was ready with another one. "This one is kind of strange. It's Matthew 18 verse ten. Jesus says not to hurt any of His little ones. He says their angels in heaven are always with God." She looked up. "Maybe it means that angels who take care of kids see God every day."

I wrote that down.

"Got it!" Donovan announced. "Verse eleven— 'God will put His angels in charge of you to protect you wherever you go.'" He smiled. "I like that. God's angels are here to protect us."

"Now look in Psalm 34, verse seven," I asked.

He found it and read it to himself. "It says almost the same thing. The angel camps around us and keeps us safe. See, I told you they're are all around us."

"You were right," I said. I looked at my note-book. "So these are the clues we have about angels from the Bible: they were created by God; they serve God and God sends them to help us; angels who take care of kids see God every day; and angels are around us all the time to protect us."

"Don't forget the times angels talked to people," Kayla reminded me. "Angels talked to the shepherds at Bethlehem when Jesus was born."

"Hey, I remember that," Donovan interrupted. "I mean, I remember that story."

Dusty joined in. "Don't forget the angel at the gate to the Garden of Eden, and the ones who talked to Abraham."

"OK," I said, writing fast. "Angels in the Bible did talk to people and give them messages. Now, what do these clues tell us about Madame LaTonn's angels?"

Donovan answered. "I think it proves that her angels are real. They talk to her, and the messages help people. That's one way of taking care of us or serving us."

Dusty agreed. "And she was right. Angels are around us all the time. Maybe she really is talking to an angel, Zack."

"Maybe so," I admitted. "Let's keep looking for clues."

Donovan was still looking at my Bible. "Hey, Zack, can I take this and show my mom? I want to tell her about the angels too."

I didn't even think about it. "Sure, Donovan. Go ahead. We'll see you later."

As he walked away, Kayla looked at me. "Do you think you'll get it back?"

Dusty was confused. "What do you mean? I thought we decided Donovan didn't steal anything."

We told him what Officer Chan had said. "But I've decided Officer Chan is wrong," I added. "I like Donovan. And I'm sure he's not a thief. We'll just have to find something that proves that to Officer Chan."

Ten minutes later, I found something that could prove just the opposite.

Angel Clues

From the Bible:

Angels talked to people in the Bible.

God created the angels.

Angels serve God and God sends them to help us.

Angels who take care of kids see God every day.

Angels are around us all the time to protect us.

Angels gave people messages in the Bible.

Madame LaTonn says the angels talk to her and give her messages. She says they're everywhere and that they're here to protect us and help us. Maybe she really is talking to angels.

Midway Mystery

Stealing has been going on at every town the fair has been to. Donovan has been around where it happened several times. He is the number-one suspect.

CHAPTER NINE

Blue Angel Answers Again

Sitting here waiting for Officer Chan, I'm not sure which mystery is more confusing—the angels or the stolen camera. None of the angel clues I have found so far prove anything about Madame LaTonn. Is she really talking to angels? Or is she making it up and pretending?

It was fun seeing how much Donovan liked reading from my Bible. But is he really a nice person, fun and honest—or is he lying to us and pretending to be nice so he can get away with stealing?

I like Donovan, but the clues keep pointing to him as the carny who is stealing from the fair visitors. Especially the latest clue.

Right after Donovan left this morning, Grandma walked out to our table.

"Hi, Grandma," Kayla said. "Want the last bite of my pickle?"

"No, thank you," Grandma answered. "I do need some help though. Zack, Dusty, could you get some things from my car for me?"

"Sure," Dusty answered for both of us. "What do you need?"

"There are two boxes in the trunk," she said. "Bring them to me in the barn. Here are my keys. Be sure and slam the trunk lid good so it locks. Thank you!" She handed Dusty the keys and turned to walk away.

"Uh, Grandma," I called after her, "where is your car parked?"

"Oh, my," she said with a laugh. "I really should tell you that. It's over that way." She waved toward the back of the parking lot. "I can't remember exactly which row, though. But that won't matter. I forget where I park so often that your grandfather gave me a special key chain. Let me show you."

Dusty handed her keys back to her. She pointed out the little button on the little box attached to her keys. "See this? It's kind of a remote control for my car. When I push it, the car's lights flash and the horn honks."

"Wow! That's cool." Dusty couldn't wait to get his hands on that remote.

"You do have to be pretty close though," she told us. "If you walk along the end of the rows and push the button, you'll see the car."

Dusty was pushing the button as soon as we got to the parking lot. "See any lights flashing?" he asked.

"Grandma said it was toward the end of the parking lot. It won't work until we get a lot closer." We kept walking until we had to step back as a big RV trailer drove slowly by. When it was past, Dusty was ready to try again.

"OK, watch and listen," he said as he pushed.

Honk, honk! From the next row over, a familiar car was flashing its lights. "There it is," Dusty announced.

When we slammed the trunk lid closed and picked up our boxes, we found ourselves following two parking lot guys. "I thought he never was going to get that RV trailer parked," one said to the other.

"I know," his friend replied. "That thing turns corners like a big box."

Something clicked in my brain. I stopped so fast Dusty ran into me. "Hey, what's going on? You almost made me drop the box."

"Oh, no! Dusty, did you hear what that guy said?"

"What guy?" Dusty asked, looking around. "The only people anywhere near us are those parking attendants. What are you talking about?"

"Come on," I said, walking as fast as I could. "We have to get to the Ferris wheel."

Dusty hurried, but I could hear him mumbling. "Ferris wheel . . . must be crazy . . . what do those parking guys know about anything?"

"Kayla," I called as soon as we were near the table, "put all that stuff back in my backpack and bring it into the barn."

"Why?" she called back. "Zack, what's going on?"

"I'll explain when we get back outside," I said over my shoulder. "Come on!"

Dusty hurried after me, but he was still mumbling. "What is it—some kind of Ferris wheel emergency?"

Finally, we left everything inside with the chickens—and Grandma and Mom. Before I had gone two steps, Kayla grabbed my arm. "What is going on? What did you find out?"

"I'll explain while we walk," I told her. "Do you remember exactly what Madame LaTonn said to

Mr. Tedrow about his camera?"

She thought for a second. "'What you have lost is in a field of big boxes, under the green.' When he didn't understand, she told him it meant that what he lost was under the big green box. But it didn't make any sense."

"It didn't to me either—until now. And I still hope I'm wrong." I turned to Dusty. "When we were riding the Ferris wheel, did you see the big place out behind the fair where all the carnies live?"

Dusty nodded. "At least I saw a place with a bunch of trailers. I figured that must be where the fair workers live. So?"

I explained. "One of those parking guys said that an RV trailer can take a long time to park because it turns like a box. So that made me remember seeing a lot of campers and RV trailers sitting out in rows in a field. "

Kayla got it. "A field of big boxes, just like Madame LaTonn said. So you think the camera is out there, under a green trailer?"

We stopped in front of the Ferris Wheel. "That's what I'm afraid of. Because when we were riding this the other night, Donovan pointed out the trailer he lives in. It's green."

"Under the big green box," Dusty repeated. "If

they find that camera under Dusty's house, he'll have a lot of explaining to do."

I agreed. "That's why we have to find it first—I want to hear him say he didn't steal it with it right in front of his face." I stood in front of the Ferris wheel and pointed off to the right. "That's the direction we were looking. Let's find a way back to the trailers."

Winding around between the game booths and rides, we found a path that led to a small gate in the chain-link fence. There was a field full of trailers, campers, and trucks. "Now, if I remember right," I said, "it should be this way. I led the way toward the center of the trailers until we found the big green one.

"So, all we have to do," Kayla said, "is walk around and look underneath the trailer. When it's not there, we'll know that the angel's riddle must have some other answer."

I walked over to begin searching at the front porch steps. The first thing I saw was a bag on the ground. It was a yellow and white bag, just like the one he was carrying the night the camera was taken.

"Uh-oh," I said out loud. "Look at this." I reached for the bag and pulled it toward us.

"Should we call Officer Chan or the security guys?" Dusty asked. "Maybe you shouldn't be touching it at all."

I knew he was right. "I'll just grab the bag by its strings. We'll open it up to look inside, but we won't touch the—whatever is inside." With one last pull, the bag slid out into the sunlight. Carefully, I pulled the top open.

"Well? What is it" Dusty asked, trying to stick his head out far enough past Kayla's. We all wanted to see into the bag.

Finally, we could see. And there in the bottom was a small camera.

"Rats," Dusty said.

"I was so sure Donovan wasn't like that," Kayla added. "I guess I was wrong."

I wasn't so sure. "There are other possibilities," I told them. "This is suspicious, but it's not proof of anything."

Then I heard a footstep behind us. "Hey, guys! What are you doing out here?" It was Donovan. He was smiling, but when he saw what we were looking at, his smile disappeared.

"So that's it," he finally said. "You were all just pretending to like me so you could 'find the thief.' I know you're not going to believe this, but I didn't steal that camera—or anything else."

Before any of us could say a word, he went inside the trailer and slammed the door.

Midway Mystery

I figured out what Madame LaTonn's message meant. It pointed right to Donovan's trailer. And that's where we found the camera.

Donovan still says he didn't steal it.

Words to Remember

RV: Recreational (rek-ree-a-shun-ul) vehicle (vee-hic-ul). Big campers that people drive when they are traveling. It's like a little house on wheels. Sometimes people use travel trailers that are like RVs except you pull them around with a truck.

CHAPTER TEN

An Accidental Clue

We walked slowly back to the midway. "What are you going to do, Zack?" Kayla asked. "Take the camera straight to Officer Chan?"

"Yeah," Dusty added glumly, "and tell him whose trailer it was under?" He shook his head. "I guess that's the right thing to do. Mr. Tedrow should get his camera back."

"I don't really want to get Donovan in trouble," I answered. "But I don't know what else we can do." None of the game booths were busy. Most of the carnies were cleaning and straightening their booths up. When I saw Donovan's mom at her booth, I thought of something. "You guys go on. I've got an idea."

They walked on toward the barn and I walked over to the basketball booth. "Hi," I said when Mrs. Davis looked up. "Remember me? I'm Zack—Donovan's friend."

She smiled. "I remember. Donovan has been talking a lot about you this week. I'm glad he found some friends. But he's not here right now. I'm sure he'll be looking for you before long."

I swallowed hard. "Well, uh, I'm not so sure. I don't know how to explain this, so I'm just going to tell you." She put down her dusting cloth and came over to stand across the counter from me. "I'm sure you know that some people think Donovan is the one stealing things at the fair."

She nodded sadly. "I know. Go on."

"The other night when we were in the back of your booth, Donovan let you think that we were his friends. The truth is, we were following him because we thought he had taken a camera."

Her face got a little less friendly. "That's why Officer Chan was following him too."

"Right," I said. "And we thought he was breaking into your booth—we didn't know you were his mom. But Donovan covered for us. And then he took us around the fair and his dad let us ride the Ferris wheel—anyway, before long, we were his friends. We still are—I hope."

A voice behind me interrupted. "Is this kid giving you any trouble, Mrs. Davis?" I turned to see Mr. Connelly—the carny from the ring-toss booth. He was smiling like Dusty's pet lizard, Ralph.

Mrs. Davis shook her head. "Customers and friends are never problems, Mr. Connelly. But thanks for asking."

He nodded. "Well, us carnies have to stick together. Have a nice day—you, too, son."

Mrs. Davis stared after him for a second, like she thought he was very confusing. Then she looked back at me. "Tell me what's happened, Zack."

I took a deep breath. "Mr. Tedrow, the man whose camera was stolen, paid Madame LaTonn to ask her angel where to find it. She gave him a strange riddle—it was under a green box in a field of big boxes. He gave up and left, but this morning I figured it out.

"There was something strange about her riddle, but I didn't have time to think about it right then." I went on.

"Anyway, Mrs. Davis, I figured out that she was talking about trailers. And Donovan had showed me your green one from the Ferris wheel. So we went there and found this under it by the porch."

I set the bag on her counter. "The camera is inside."

She closed her eyes. Tears squeezed out from the corners. "So why didn't you just take it to Officer Chan?" she asked.

"Because Donovan is my friend. Because if I might be in this kind of trouble, my mom would want to know."

Her eyes were still wet, but she smiled at me. "Thank you, Zack, for being his friend. I know this all looks bad, but I'm just certain that Donovan is not taking these things. He's not that kind of person. He's kind and honest." She reached out and pushed the bag toward me. "Take this to Officer Chan. Tell him everything you told me. Donovan has done nothing wrong, and we have nothing to hide."

Then the curtains to the back of the tent moved and someone stepped out. "I'll go with you," a voice said. It was Donovan!

Then his mother had her arms around him and he hugged her just as hard. "I promise I didn't take that camera or anything else, Mom. I really didn't."

"We'll figure it out, dear," she said. "We'll find a way to prove you aren't stealing these things."

"We will," I added. "I promise. Come on, let's get started."

After a few more hugs, we headed out to find

Officer Chan. "Sorry about what I said at the trailer," Donovan told me. "I even thought maybe you guys had put the camera there to make it look like I did it. Thanks for believing me."

"That's what friends are for," I said. "Now we just have to figure out who is doing the stealing, so we can convince Officer Chan." Our path led to the back side of the security building.

As we walked around, Donovan stopped me with one hand and held the other to his lips. "Shhh! Listen."

Around the front of the building, someone was talking to Officer Chan. "You've got to do something about these young hooligans! I had more things stolen just this morning. Nothing expensive, mind you, but stolen right out from under my nose! It's getting to where a person can't close his eyes for a second."

Officer Chan's voice was calm. "We're doing everything we can. If you'll report these things when they happen, we'll have a much better chance of catching the person—young or old—before they leave the fair."

The other voice got quieter also. "I think we both know who's doing it, Officer. The same kid who stole that camera. You'd better keep an eye on him!"

We both peeked around the corner to see who was so upset. It was Mr. Connelly. "Hey," I whispered, "I thought he liked you. He told your mom that carnies have to stick together."

Donovan shook his head. "I don't trust him. I think he acts nice to us because Dad's his boss." When Mr. Connelly left, we stepped around to the front. Officer Chan was ready to leave. "Hi, boys," he said. "Staying out of trouble?"

"Yes," I answered. "And helping you, too. We found this for you." When I set the bag on his counter, he sat back down and opened it.

"Is this what I think it is?" he asked. He reached for his notepad and compared Mr. Tedrow's report to the camera in the bag. Then he nodded. "That's the stolen camera." He looked at Donovan. "Did you decide to bring it back?"

I answered for Donovan. "No, he didn't. I found it by figuring out Madame LaTonn's message to Mr. Tedrow."

Officer Chan looked surprised. "You figured it out? Tell me how."

So I explained it all again. "And it was right there, under their trailer, next to the porch."

"Good thinking," he said. "Maybe that Madame LaTonn really does talk to angels. Donovan, do you have any idea how the camera got there?"

"No, sir," Donovan said. "I've never stolen any-thing. That's why I wanted to come with Zack to bring it to you. I want to help find whoever did steal it."

Officer Chan stroked his chin. "You know that it looks very suspicious to find the camera at your house." Donovan just hung his head.

"That's true," I agreed. "But why would he steal it just to throw it on the ground in plain sight? If he was just doing it for fun, he certainly wouldn't throw it away at his own house. And if he wanted to keep it, he'd have hidden it inside somewhere." Donovan nodded.

Officer Chan sighed. "You have a good point. OK, if you boys will help me by keeping your eyes open and reporting anything you see, I'll keeping looking for other answers. Now, let's call Mr. Tedrow."

As he dialed the phone, I looked at Donovan. He was grinning. "Officer Chan is a nice guy after all. But we have to figure this out before the fair ends, or people will always believe I did it—people like Mr. Connelly."

"Hello, Mr. Tedrow? We found your camera. Yes, it appears that the film is still inside." Officer Chan held it up to look. "Looks like you're at the end of a roll of twenty-four shots." He listened for a moment. "Oh, really? That could prove most interesting."

He put his hand over the receiver and spoke to us. "Mr. Tedrow says that he had only taken twenty-three pictures. Maybe the thief accidently snapped the last picture on the roll. That could give us a clue."

CHAPTER ELEVEN

Angel Boss

Well, the chicken judging is over. Agatha won the blue ribbon! And Esmeralda? Well, I think the judges must have been looking for chickens with good personalities—and she wasn't smart enough to hide hers. The way I hear it, not only did she not win—she was lucky to get away without being plucked!

I can tell she blames it on me.

But she's home now, scratching in the dirt and I'm here at my table scratching in this notebook. Officer Chan sent in the film from Mr. Tedrow's camera to be developed. When it comes back, we'll find out whether or not our accidental clue is helpful.

DETECTIVE ZACK

But I do have other clues to write down—clues about angels. We learned more this morning when we read some stories from the Bible. Actually, it started last night.

After we got home, I had some soup in the kitchen with Mom and Grandpa. I decided not to tell them about Donovan and the accidental clue in the camera—at least not until we saw the picture. But Mom wanted to know about the other mystery.

"So how did you search for angel clues go, Zack?" she asked.

"We found a lot of them," I answered after I swallowed. "Angels are all around us to protect us. They work for God and He sends them to help us. They give messages to people. But there's still something I don't understand. Can we talk to our angel? Can we ask for help or answers? Angels seemed to talk to people in Bible times a lot."

Grandpa nodded as he stirred his soup. "Like the Christmas story where the angels talked to the shepherds?"

"Right," I answered. "And when the angels came to Abraham's tent."

"All right," he said, "Think about why the angels appeared and spoke to people."

I thought. "Well, of course the Christmas angels

came to announce that Jesus was born. No one asked them to come—except God. He sent them down to earth."

Grandpa had a spoonful of soup. "Go on," he said. "Why did the angels visit Abraham?"

"Well, they had something to tell him. About Abraham and his wife having a baby, and about Sodom being destroyed."

"So they were there to answer questions Abraham had asked them?"

"Well, no." I frowned at my soup. "They brought him a message from God. Didn't God come with the angels?"

"That's right," Grandpa said. "And then God sent the angels on to Sodom. When Abraham heard that Sodom would be destroyed, what did he do?"

I knew this one. "He asked God not to destroy it."

Grandpa's eyes twinkled. "Why didn't he ask the angels not to? They were the ones who were going there."

Something was starting to click in my brain. "Because the angels were doing what God told them to do."

Grandpa nodded. "You already found this clue in your Bible. You told me that angels serve God and that God sends them to help us."

I was getting it. "So, in the Bible, people ask God for help or answers. Then He may send angels to help."

Grandpa put his soup bowl in the sink. "Why don't you look up the stories for yourself? I'll give you some chapters and verses to read, and then you can decide what happened with angels in the Bible."

So this morning, I brought his list and we sat at the table near the barn again to search for more angel clues in our Bibles. Donovan brought my Bible back, so he used that. "OK, Kayla. You look up the angel story in Numbers chapter 22. Dusty, you look in Second Kings chapter 6. Donovan, you find Acts 12."

"Oh, I like this story," Kayla said when she found hers. "It's the one about Balaam. You know, he's riding his donkey to a spot so he can curse God's people. But an angel stands in the path so the donkey keeps turning away and stopping. Finally, God let the donkey talk, so it said, "Why are you beating me?"

Dusty laughed. "And Balaam was so mad he started arguing with his donkey!"

Donovan's mouth fell open. "No way! Is that story really in there?"

"Sure," Kayla answered. "Then, God let Balaam see the angel that his donkey was seeing and he fell on the ground. But he listened to what God wanted him to do."

Donovan shook his head. "That's stranger than the stuff Madame LaTonn does."

I agreed. "It's weird, all right. But something about it is different. So what's the clue about angels in this story?" I asked.

Kayla had an idea. "Well, this angel didn't come to answer a question Balaam had. It showed up to give him a message—a message from God."

"Listen to my story," Dusty insisted. "This country Syria was fighting against Israel and they wanted to capture the prophet Elisha. So they came and surrounded the city. When Elisha's servant saw the army, he was scared to death. Elisha said, 'Don't worry. Our army is bigger.' Then he prayed that God would let the servant see the army of angels around them. The servant was amazed."

Donovan was amazed too. "A whole army of angels came because Elisha asked for it?"

"Sounds like it," I said. "But look who he asked. Not the angels—he asked God."

Donovan started to say something, but he found his story instead. "It says that some guy named

Peter was in prison and everyone was praying for him. So an angel appeared and led him right out of prison without waking anyone else up." He thought for a second. "The people asked God for help, so God sent an angel."

I had an idea. "Donovan, when it's time to set up the rides and booths at a new fair, your dad's in charge, right?"

Donovan sat up straight and smiled. "That's right."

"So, what if someone has a problem or needs help?" I asked.

"They ask Dad."

I grinned. "But what if they just ask one of the carnies to stop and help them?"

Donovan shook his head. "That carny should point to Dad and say 'He's the boss. Ask him.'" Then he thought for a second. "You're saying that God is like the angel Boss. Anyone who needs help or wants answers needs to ask Him. Then He sends the angel."

"That's the way it happens in the Bible," I agreed.

"And in real life, too," Kayla said suddenly. "Zack, remember those two angels we saw on our trip?"

Donovan's eyes almost popped out. "You saw

real angels? How?"

"We think they were angels," I said. "We were on our trip to find clues about Noah's Flood in Utah. But our van didn't run well in those high mountains. Finally, one night when we were heading back to our camp, the van stopped. It was almost dark, and we were out in a desert."

Kayla jumped in. "Remember, if we had only made it over one more hill, we could have coasted all the way back. But we didn't make it. Dad tried a few things, then we prayed and asked God to help us."

I went on. "Right after that, I saw headlights coming up the road behind us. A junky old station wagon pulled up and the scruffy looking guys inside asked if we needed help."

Kayla almost shivered. "They looked like they had been off camping or hunting for weeks with those dirty, ragged clothes and that wild hair."

"They offered to push our car from behind with their bumper," I said. "Dad was afraid that their car would really smash up the back of ours. But the bumper on their car was exactly the same height as the back bumper on our van. So Dad got in, and they started pushing. They pushed us all the way up the hill, then we coasted ahead of them going down the other side."

"I was watching them too," Kayla added. "They got farther and farther behind, then suddenly their headlights disappeared."

Donovan looked confused. "How do you know they didn't just turn off on another road?"

"There weren't any roads." I said. "The first road we came to was the one we turned on, to the place we were staying. When we got out, our car wasn't dented at all. And we decided that maybe those were two angels God sent to help us— dressed like ragged hunters."

Donovan was quiet for a few seconds. Then he pointed to the Blue Angel booth. "So if she's not talking to angels and getting answers from them, what's going on over there?"

"That's what we have to find out," I said.

Angel Clues

From the Bible:

In the story of Balaam, the angel came to bring a message from God, not because Balaam asked for help.

A whole army of angels came when Elisha needed protection from the Syrian army. But Elisha didn't ask the angels for help—he asked God for help.

When Peter was in prison, his friends prayed that God would save him. Then an angel appeared and led him out. The people asked God for help, and God sent an angel.

Maybe God is like the angel Boss. Whenever someone needs help or answers, they ask God. Then God sends an angel to help.

That's how it happened to us on our trip. When our car broke down, we prayed for help. The people who showed up and helped us may have been angels!

CHAPTER TWELVE

Setting the Trap

We all stared across the roadway at the Blue Angel booth. While we watched, a woman stood by the window as the blue angel glowed. Then she got an answer and walked away smiling.

"If she's not talking to an angel," Dusty asked, "how do you explain the blue angel glowing when she puts her hands on it and asks a question?"

"I don't know," I said. "But there's got to be a way to find out. Do you think she'll let us inside the booth?"

"No way," Kayla answered. "Sonia tried that. Madame LaTonn said that if anyone else came in, it would mess up her way of talking to the angel."

Donovan agreed. "She never lets anyone in."

"Are you sure?" I asked. "I thought someone went out the back door of her booth that first morning when we were asking her about Zippy."

Donovan shrugged. "Maybe it was someone who helped her set the booth up. All I know is, she never leaves the booth with anyone else. Either she's there, or it's closed."

Before we could come up with anything else, Officer Chan walked up. "Well, we have the pictures back. And here is that extra one that the thief took." He held up a photograph.

"Well?" I needed some answers. "What does it show? Is it a clue?"

Officer Chan frowned. "Well, it's a clue, I guess. But not a very good one. Here, see for yourselves." He handed the picture to me. Then three heads clunked into mine.

"Ow," I complained.

"Sorry," Kayla said, rubbing her head. "We want to see too."

All the picture showed was one part of the edge of a blue cloth. Along that edge, you could see light. "It's a curtain," Officer Chan answered before we could ask. "All of the game booths and many others in the fair have this same blue curtain hanging up to block off the back where the supplies are kept."

Dusty frowned. "So anyone could have accidently snapped that while they were walking by a booth. Even Mr. Tedrow might have done it."

"No," I said. I was still looking at the photograph. "See the light around the edge? Whoever took this was inside a booth looking out. The camera caught the sunlight around the edge of the curtain."

Donovan looked again. "You're right. This could have been taken right from the back of my mom's booth." Then he thought about what he was saying and turned a little red. Officer Chan stared at him. Donovan went on quickly, "I said it could have. It wasn't. At least, I didn't take it. And I know my mom didn't." He stopped and shook his head. "Oh, great. A clue that makes you think I did it. Now we'll never find out who the real thief is." He walked away. "I'll see you guys later."

Officer Chan sat down with us. "He's right, you know. At least the clue does make it seem even more likely that the thief is one of the carnies—someone who can go behind the curtain in a booth in daylight."

I frowned. "But it would be really stupid for him to say that if he took the camera. And Donovan is not stupid."

"You're right," Officer Chan agreed. "None of

the clues prove he did it. But all the clues say he could have done it. So for now, he's still the top suspect."

I smacked the table with my hand. "We need a way to track the thief. What we need is a trap."

Kayla put her hands up. "Look out! When he puts together a trap, there's always trouble."

"Trouble?" Officer Chan asked.

Dusty stood up and backed away. "Remind me to tell you about the one with the skunk," he said.

"Hey, my traps always work," I said. "Some just don't work the first time."

Just then Grandma walked up. "Hello, Officer," she said. "These kids aren't giving you any trouble, are they?"

"No," he answered with a laugh. "Actually, they're trying to help." He stood up. "I'd better be going. Let me know about that trap, Zack."

While Grandma talked to Kayla, she jingled her keys in her hand. Suddenly, I had a great idea. "Grandma, can I borrow your keys for just a minute?"

"Sure, dear." She handed them to me and I took off after Officer Chan. He stopped when I slid in front of him.

"I have a plan for a trap," I said before he could speak. "What we need is a way to get them to steal something we can track and follow, right?"

"Well, sure," he agreed. "But that's not easy."

I held up Grandma's key chain. "What if we use something like this? It helps my Grandma find her car when she can't remember when she parked it. When she gets close, she pushes this button, the car horn honks and the lights flash."

"I've seen these," he said as he took the key chain and looked at the remote. "We could make a small beeper work like that. But what would we put it in?"

Suddenly someone crashed into my back. "Sorry," the man said as he lowered his video camera. "I was walking backward to get a tape of her riding in her stroller." He smiled at his little girl and his wife who was pushing the stroller.

"Try to be careful," Officer Chan said as they walked away.

I pointed to the video camera. "What if we put the beeper in one of those? I could carry it around all afternoon and evening to make sure everyone saw it, then 'accidently' leave it where it could be stolen."

Officer Chan smiled and handed me back the keys. "That might work, Zack. I'll go put something together. You ask your parents if you can carry it. I'll be back on duty here at six o'clock.

Bring your mom or dad to the security booth around then so I can talk to them." He started to walk away, then stopped. "One more thing, Zack. If we do this, you can't tell Donovan about it. I know you believe him, but if he is lying, this might be my best chance to catch him."

I frowned. "OK. I won't tell him."

By the time I explained the plan about a hundred times to Dusty and Kayla and Mom and Grandma, it was time to meet Officer Chan. I introduced him to Mom, then let them talk.

"I'm sure Zack will be in no danger," he said. "No one's been hurt in any of the thefts at the fair. And I or the another security officer will be close by no matter where he goes. I appreciate Zack's wanting to help me solve this. I know he's trying to help a friend too."

Mom smiled nervously. "I guess it will be OK. Kayla and Dusty are going to stay with you—right, Zack?"

"Right," I answered. "Now, where's the camera?"

Officer Chan pulled a small video camera out from under the counter. "This is damaged. Nothing in it works except the viewer. So it will look like you are filming on tape, but nothing will be recorded. We replaced the recording device with a beeper tuned to this remote." He held up a small box with a short antenna.

Dusty leaned in to look closer at the camera. "How do you turn it on?" he asked. "Oh, here it is— the power button."

Officer Chan finished what he was saying. "If the camera is stolen, we'll walk around the fair and press this button. When we are close to the video camera, it will beep like this." He pushed the button.

BEEP! BEEP! BEEP!

Dusty jumped back three feet and plastered his hands over his ears. "Wow! That's loud!"

Officer Chan shut it off. "We wanted to be sure it could be heard over the noise of the fair. Zack, if nothing happens, just bring it back here when you leave. If the camera disappears, grab the first security person you see and tell them to find me quick!"

I looped the camera strap around my neck and picked up the fake camera. "OK," I said to Kayla and Dusty, "let's go catch the bad guys."

Angel Clues

If Madame LaTonn is not really talking to angels, what is she doing? Why does that blue light glow every time she puts her hands on the angel statue?

Words to Remember

Video camera: Camera that records video pictures you can watch on your VCR at home.

Midway Mystery

The accidental photograph was a picture of one edge of a curtain in a booth. And it had to be taken looking out from inside. So someone who goes inside a booth—a carny—must have taken it.

This clue points to Donovan again.

We're setting a trap that might work!

CHAPTER THIRTEEN

One More Question

"Get a picture of that, Zack," Kayla called from across the midway. She pointed to the Ferris wheel. Now that the lights were on, it was a pretty picture. I aimed the video camera at it and stared.

This was our second trip down the midway. We just walked along, taking turns holding the camera up like we were filming the whole fair.

"Hey, nice video camera," a voice behind me said. It was Donovan.

"Want to try it?" I asked. "Just look through here." I handed it to him and he focused on his dad by the Ferris wheel.

Dusty grabbed at my sleeve. "I thought Donovan

wasn't supposed to know about it," he hissed in my ear.

"He doesn't know it's a fake," I whispered back. "Besides, if he's with us, he can't be accused of stealing anything."

After walking the rest of the way down the midway and back, I decided it was time to set the camera down and see if someone would take it. "Let's get some ice cream," I suggested. "We can buy cones at that place down by the corn-on-the-cob booth." By the time we waited in line and bought our cones, I really was tired of the camera. I wanted it off my neck.

I led the way to a table next to a row of bushes. Kayla, Dusty, and I all sat on one side of the table, facing out toward the Ferris wheel. I set the camera down on the ground behind us. When Donovan started to sit across from us, I wasn't sure what to do. But I didn't need to do anything.

"Hey, Donovan," a teenage carny called. "I'm supposed to tell you that your mom's looking for you."

"OK," Donovan called back. "She probably just wants to check on me," he told us. "I'll be right back."

"So we just sit here and wait for someone to take it," Kayla asked quietly.

"That's right," I answered. "And if they don't, we go somewhere else and sit."

While we licked our ice cream, a man on stilts walked by, looking like a cowboy with twenty-foot-long legs. "I wish I could walk on stilts like that," Dusty said. "I'd be the best basketball player in school."

The tall man waved and disappeared behind a tree. Then, we heard him yell. "Whoa! Look out!"

"Do you think he fell down?" Kayla was worried.

Dusty jumped up. "Let's go see."

I was right behind them. We found the stilt-walker hanging on to a tree limb, trying to stand up again. "Now that's a good picture," I said to Kayla. Then I remembered. "I forgot the camera!" I ran back to our table, but the camera was gone.

"Quick," I called to Dusty and Kayla, "find a security person. The camera's gone!"

"Here comes two of them." Dusty pointed down the roadway. "And one of them is Officer Chan."

He saw us waving our arms, but checked on the stilt-walker first. "You take care of this," he told his partner. Then he turned to us. "It's gone?" We all nodded. "Then let's go find it," he said as he pulled the remote out of his pocket.

As we walked down the midway, Officer Chan stopped in front of each booth and pushed the button. We hadn't gone far when Donovan ran up laughing. "Hey, did you guys hear about that stilt-walker who fell into the tree?" Then he saw Officer Chan. "What happened?"

"Someone stole our video camera," I said.

He looked at the remote. "And you're going to find it with that?"

I explained. "The camera was a trap. There's a beeper hidden inside. When we get close enough to it and he pushes that button, the beeper is going to go off—and it's very loud. We'll find the thief this time."

Donovan blinked. "Good idea. Can I come along?"

"No problem," Officer Chan said as we walked to the next booth. No beeps there either. Before long, we were in front of the basketball game booth. I held my breath just for a second when Officer Chan pushed the button. But nothing beeped.

Finally, we reached the end of the midway. "That's it," Dusty said. "There's nowhere else to go."

"Just one more place," Officer Chan announced. "Donovan, I think we should go check at your trailer."

Donovan swallowed hard, but he nodded. "Let's go. I don't have anything to hide."

"You don't think he really stole it, do you?" Kayla whispered to me as we walked.

I wanted to say no. But I said, "He wasn't with us when it was stolen. He could have taken it. This way, we'll know."

"But what if someone else hid it there, like last time?" she asked. I didn't have any answer to that.

We walked to the front porch and stopped while Officer Chan pushed the button and walked around the trailer. Donovan had his fingers crossed. Kayla had her eyes closed. I tried to remember why I thought this was a good idea.

But nothing happened. Officer Chan walked back to us and said, "Let's go." We were happy to leave. "I guess we won't catch the thief tonight," he said. "Maybe it really was a visitor this time. Maybe we just weren't lucky. Anyway, it was a good idea, Zack."

Dusty snorted. "What did I tell you about his traps? They always go wrong."

"Thanks for trying, Zack," Donovan said.

I frowned, but I wasn't listening to them. "We didn't solve either one of our mysteries," I said. "Officer Chan, do you believe that Madame LaTonn talks to angels?"

He shook his head. "No, I don't. She just tells people what they really want to hear, like any fortune-teller does."

Kayla nodded. "That's what I heard one man call her—a fortune-teller. She gave that one woman a message that sounded like a wedding. But it could have been a funeral."

"That's the way these people work," Officer Chan said. "A young woman comes and asks about the future, and they tell her something that might mean she'll go to a wedding. Well, anyone could guess that she'll be at her own wedding or one of her friends' weddings before long. And the fortune-teller can't really be wrong—they'll just say you didn't understand the message right."

"But what about that blue angel light?" Dusty asked. "How does she do that?"

"I don't know," Officer Chan admitted.

"And what about the messages we figured out?" Kayla asked. "How did she know where Sonia's hamster and that camera were?"

"Maybe she just got lucky," Donovan suggested.

"Maybe," Officer Chan said. "Or maybe you would have looked in those spots anyway, and the message just made you keep trying."

I wasn't so sure. "I never would have figured out where the camera was if she hadn't explained that part about it being under a green box." Before I took another step, something in my brain clicked.

"Wait a minute," I said, stopping by the light of the baseball throwing booth. "Officer Chan, do you still have that picture?"

He patted his top pocket, then pulled the picture out. "Why?" he asked as he handed it over.

I studied it again—the blue curtain and the light around the edge. "That's it!" I declared. "Come on. I have a question for Madame LaTonn."

They hurried after me, but they were confused. "Zack, you decided that she's just a fake!" Kayla said. "Why are you going to ask her a question now?"

"You'll see," I answered. When we got close to the Blue Angel booth, I turned to Officer Chan. "Can I hold the remote for a minute? And would you wait over here, by the side?"

He started to argue, then didn't. "It's worth a try," was all he said.

I marched around to the window, with the other three right behind me. After the woman in front of us left, I plopped three dollar bills on the counter. "I want to ask a question."

Madame LaTonn scooped the money into a drawer. "You may ask," she said.

I took a deep breath. "My video camera was stolen tonight. Where is it?"

She closed her eyes and touched the blue statue.

DETECTIVE ZACK

The blue light seemed brighter than ever. Finally, she spoke. "What you seek is in darkness, rolling away quickly."

"What does that mean?" I asked.

She shook her head. "That is all the angel told me. I never try to explain their messages."

I just had one more question.

Angel Clues

Officer Chan doesn't believe Madame LaTonn talks to angels either. He says she's just like other fortune-tellers—they tell you something that could mean a lot of different things.

He thinks we found Zippy and the camera because we kept thinking and looking, not because of her message. Or else she just made a lucky guess.

We still don't how what creates the blue angel light.

Words to Remember

Fortune-teller: A person who claims they can tell you what will happen before it does. They usually answer people's questions for money.

Stilt-walker: A person who has learned how to walk on tall sticks call stilts. Sometimes stilt-walkers wear costumes.

CHAPTER FOURTEEN

The Real Answers

I pulled out another three dollars and put it on Madame LaTonn's counter. "Then I have one more question."

She gave me a puzzled look, then scooped the money away. "You may ask," she said again.

I set the remote up on the counter. "What will happen if I press this button?" Then before she could say a word, I pressed it.

BEEP! BEEP! BEEP!

The booth almost exploded with the sound. Madame LaTonn put her hands over her ears and screamed something no one could hear. Then the back door flew open and someone ran out—right into Officer Chan's arms. I ran around to the back, pushed the button again and the sound stopped.

"Hold it right there," Officer Chan said to his captive. "I think you have some explaining to do."

Donovan was right beside me. When he saw who Officer Chan was holding, he was shocked. "Mr. Connelly! You stole the video camera?"

"He stole more than that," I said. "Look!" The back of the booth was lined with things—the video camera, some radios, a walkie-talkie, and two regular cameras in their cases.

Officer Chan took one look and grabbed his radio. "Headquarters, I need assistance on an arrest. Send all available officers to the Blue Angel booth."

As soon as the first officer arrived, Officer Chan handed Mr. Connelly to her. Then he went inside the booth and pushed the blue curtain back. "Madame LaTonn—or whatever your name really is—you need to come with me." She stood up and walked out without saying a word. Another officer took her by the arm.

"Zack, how did you know?" Kayla asked. She was staring in through the window at the front.

"Wait a second," I told her. When Madame LaTonn was out, I stepped in. "Just one more mystery to solve." Officer Chan raised one eyebrow, but he stepped back and let me walk to the front. I looked at the blue angel, then looked underneath the counter where it stood. "Watch this," I said.

While everyone watched, I put my hands on the blue angel. Suddenly, it began to glow, just like before. This time, Dusty's mouth fell open so far, the blue light made his tonsils glow. "How—how did you do that?" he stammered.

"It's simple," I said. "And it has nothing to do with my hands. There's a switch on the floor attached to a bright lamp directly underneath the angel statue. When you step on the switch, the light comes on slowly, then very bright, then it shuts off. Like this." I stepped on the switch, then stepped away. The angel glowed just like before.

Dusty swallowed. "I guess your traps aren't always a disaster," he admitted. I just smiled.

Before it was over last night, I explained it to everyone. "When we were walking back from the trailer, I talked about Madame LaTonn's message to Mr. Tedrow. But I finally noticed what I said—when he didn't understand, she explained some of it to him."

"That's right," Kayla remembered. "She explained the 'under the green' meant 'under the big green box.' But she told us that she never explained her messages."

I nodded my head. "That's why I asked her to explain my message about the video camera. I could tell that she was trying to make me think that the video camera was in the trunk of someone's car and gone. But then she said it again—'I never explain.' Why would she have explained to Mr. Tedrow unless she wanted to be sure he found the camera?"

"And blamed it on me," Donovan said.

"Right." I agreed. "Anyway, when I remembered that, I looked at the photograph clue again. If she was involved in stealing the camera, what did the photograph show?"

Officer Chan held it up to look at again. "That's not daylight around the edge of the curtain. It's blue light from the angel." He shook his head. "It's easy to see that now."

"Donovan," I asked, "remember when I said I saw someone go out the back door of that booth the first morning?" He nodded. "I think Madame LaTonn and Mr. Connelly must have been trying to get more business and to make sure everyone thought she was nice and helpful."

Kayla nodded. "He probably found Zippy while we were looking for him. Then he told her where he was going to hide the hamster. When we started asking, he snuck out the back and put

Zippy under the box."

"The two of them must have been working together all this time. Mr. Connelly stole the things and hid them in her booth so she could take them out and sell them after the fair. Madame LaTonn helped people find some things—the ones she didn't want to keep or sell—to make it look like she was helping the security officers."

Officer Chan shook his head. "We did think she was helping. Boy, did she have us fooled. They worked hard to make me think that Donovan was the thief. Connelly even came over and complained to me about him. They tricked me. I'm sorry, Donovan."

"It's OK," Donovan said. "He was fooling the carnies too. And stealing from them."

"I didn't know who was helping her," I admitted. "I just hoped whoever it was would be inside when the beeper went off."

This morning, I had to explain most of it again for Mom and Grandma. And for Donovan's parents. "Thank you for being a friend to Donovan," Mrs. Davis said. "I don't know what would have happened if you guys hadn't figured this out."

Mom smiled and patted my arm. "So this is where all those questions about angels came from. Did you find the answers you were looking for?"

I nodded, but Donovan answered. "We know that angels get their orders from God. People who need help or have questions have to ask God. Then God can send an angel."

His mom looked surprised. "Donovan, you've learned a lot this week."

I looked at Mom. She pulled something out of her bag and handed it to me. "Donovan," I said, "since we won't see you much after today, we want you to have this." I handed him a new Bible.

His eyes got really big. "It's mine? To keep?"

"There are a lot of great stories in there," Kayla said. "And a lot of great people. You'll like reading it."

"Thank you," he said, opening the pages to look inside. "Thank you very much."

Now that the fair is over, and most of Grandpa's house is fixed, we'll be heading for home. It's almost time for school to start anyway. Maybe that's a good thing. I thought I knew all about angels before. But I didn't know enough to know that Madame LaTonn was a fake right away. Maybe there are other things in the Bible I need to learn more about.

Oh, one last thing. When we said goodbye, Donovan said, "I just wish I could see an angel sometime like you guys did."

"Well, we think we did," I said. "Besides, you might see an angel anytime."

He was confused. "Really? How?"

I laughed. "Look up Hebrews chapter thirteen, verse two, in your Bible and see!"

I hope Donovan gets to see a real angel some-day. I hope I do too!

Angel Clues

Angels are really around us all the time. God sent them to protect us and help us—when we ask God for help.

When angels talk to people, they are bringing a message from God.

Angels don't work apart from God—they work for God.

Grandpa told me that fortune-tellers and people like them are either faking it or they're trying to work with the devil. He said the best thing for a Christian is just to stay away from them. I think he's right!

The Last Answer

"Remember to welcome strangers in your homes. There are some who did that and welcomed angels without knowing it," (Hebrews 13:2, TEV).